SHOW AND SPELL

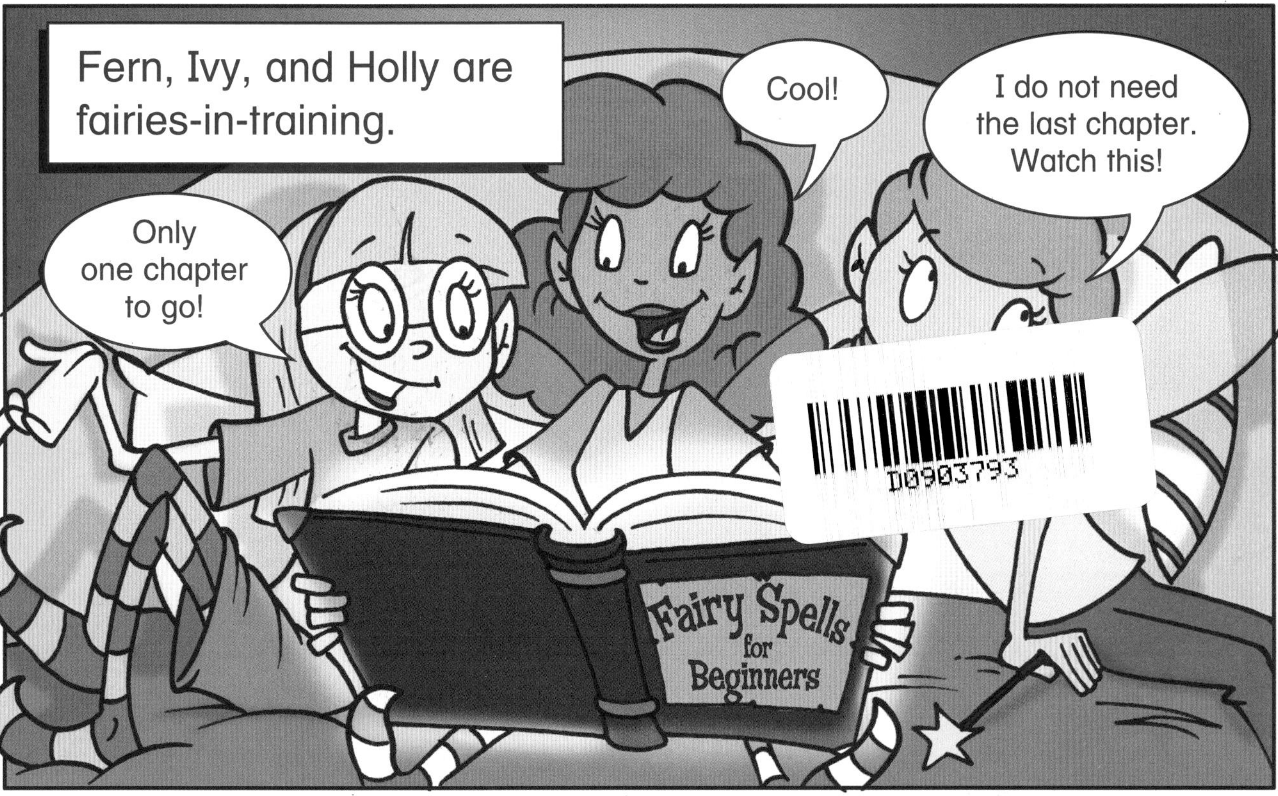
Fern, Ivy, and Holly are fairies-in-training.
Only one chapter to go!
Cool!
I do not need the last chapter. Watch this!
Fairy Spells for Beginners

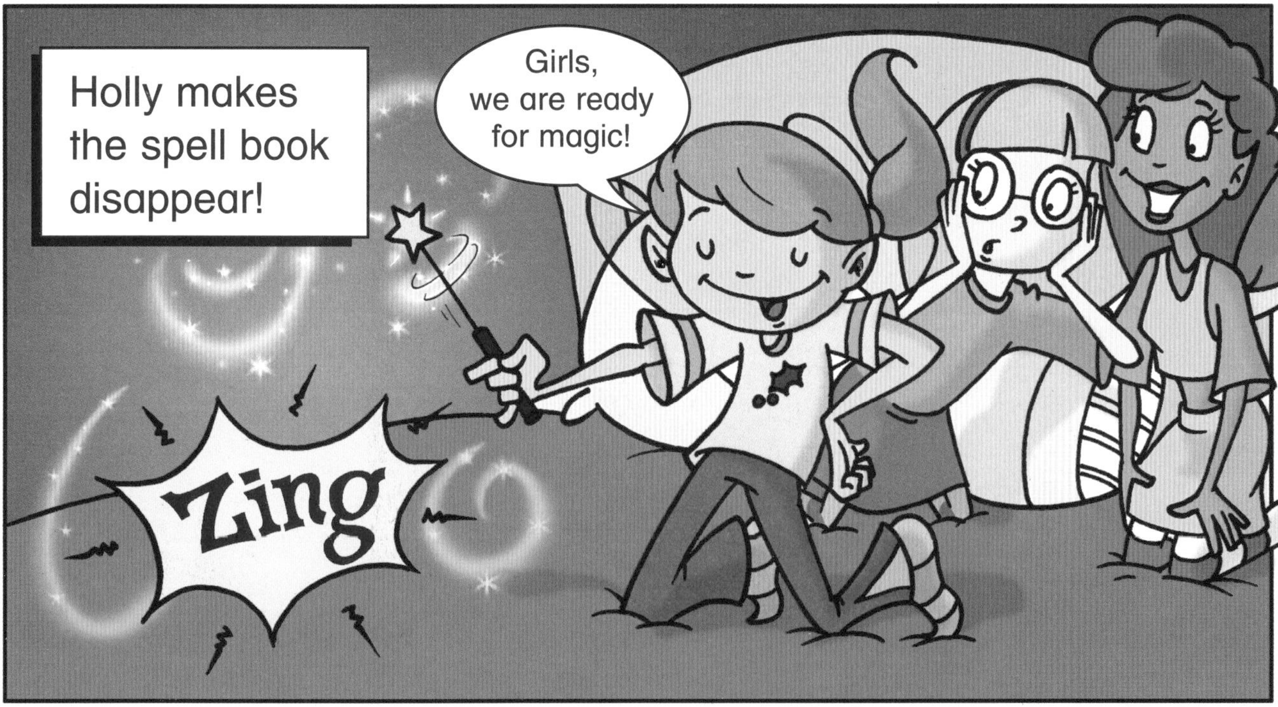
Holly makes the spell book disappear!
Girls, we are ready for magic!
Zing

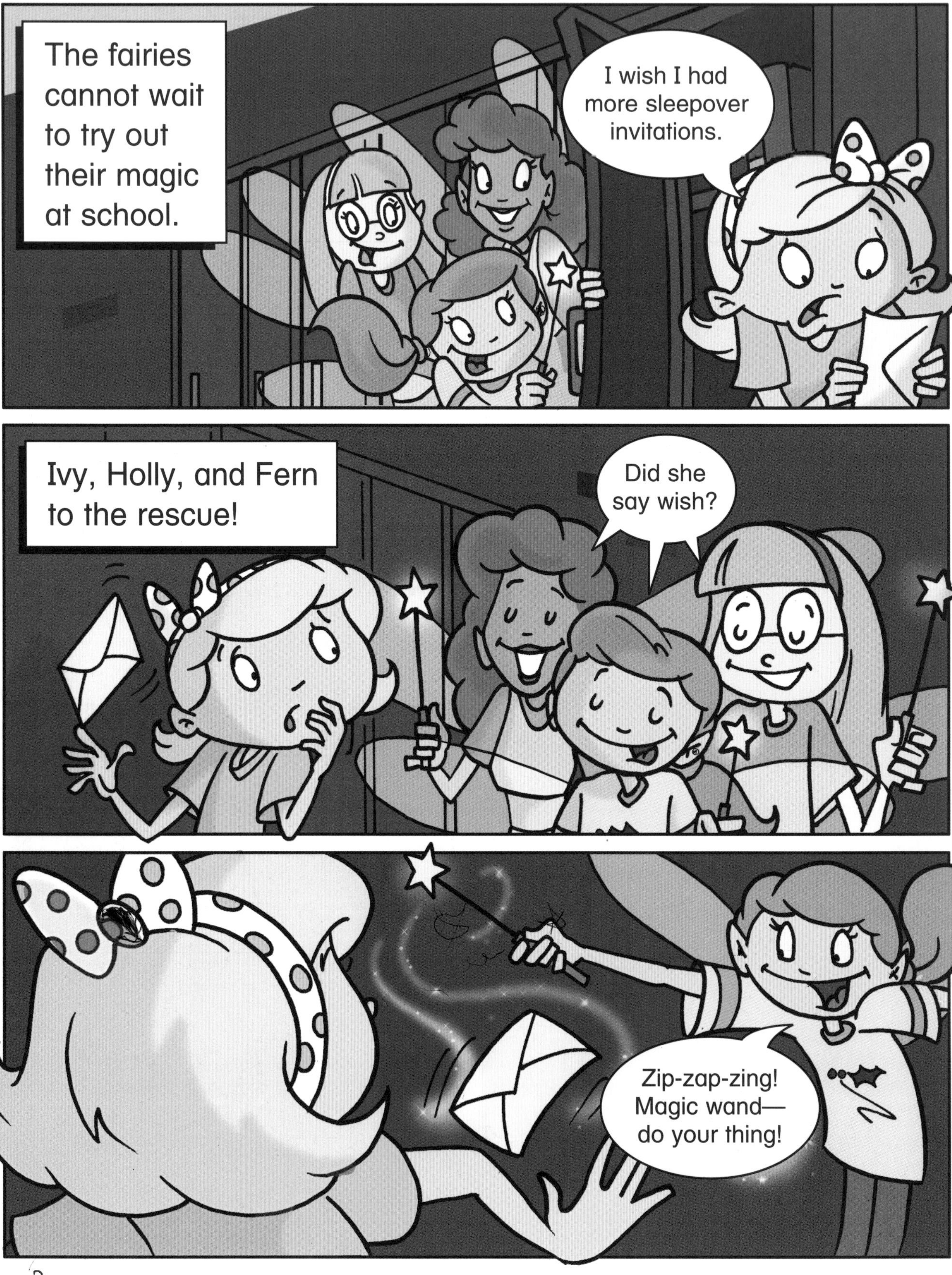
The fairies cannot wait to try out their magic at school.
I wish I had more sleepover invitations.
Ivy, Holly, and Fern to the rescue!
Did she say wish?
Zip-zap-zing! Magic wand— do your thing!

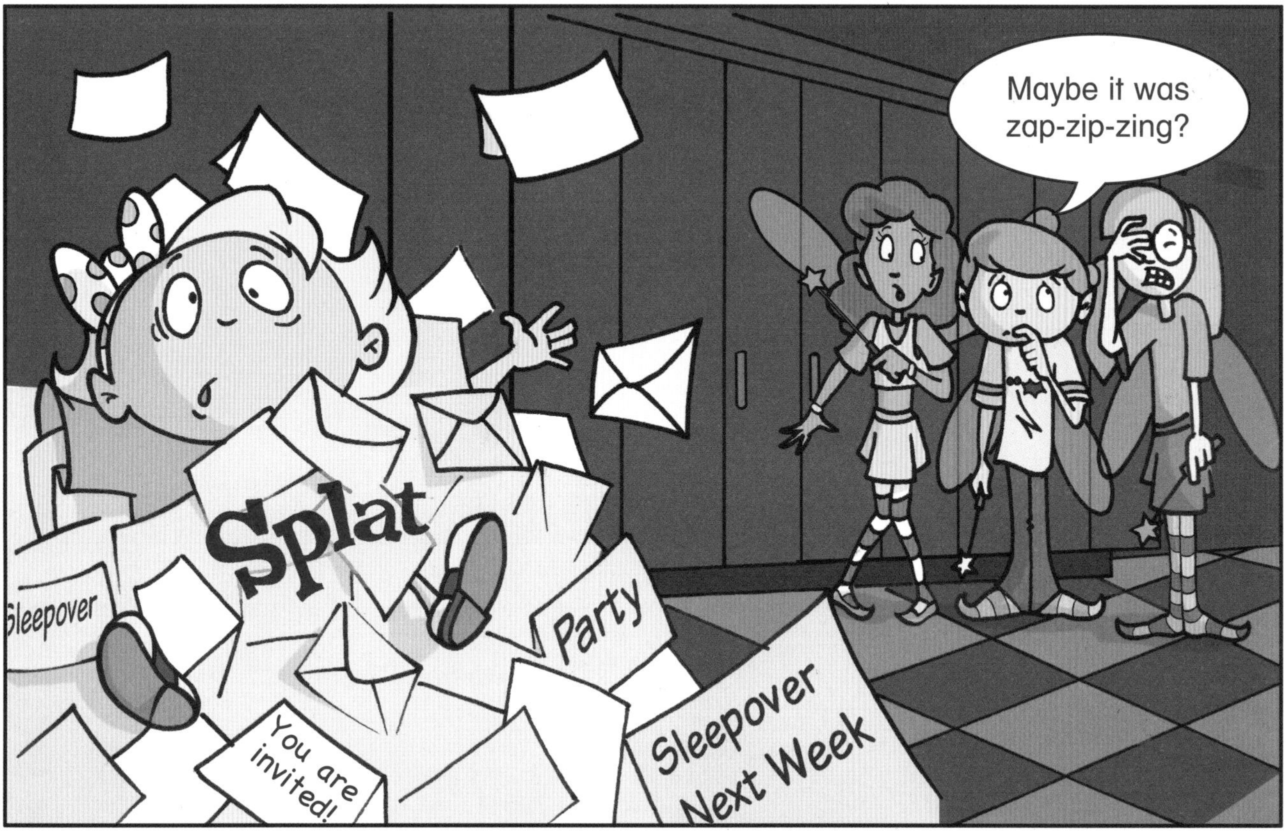
Maybe it was zap-zip-zing?
Splat
Sleepover
Party
You are invited!
Sleepover Next Week

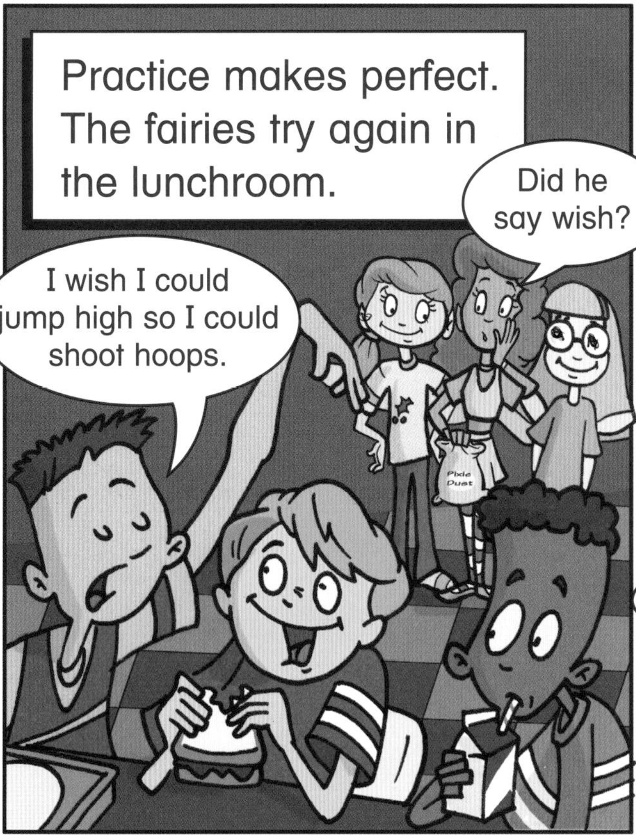
Practice makes perfect. The fairies try again in the lunchroom.
Did he say wish?
I wish I could jump high so I could shoot hoops.
Pixie Dust

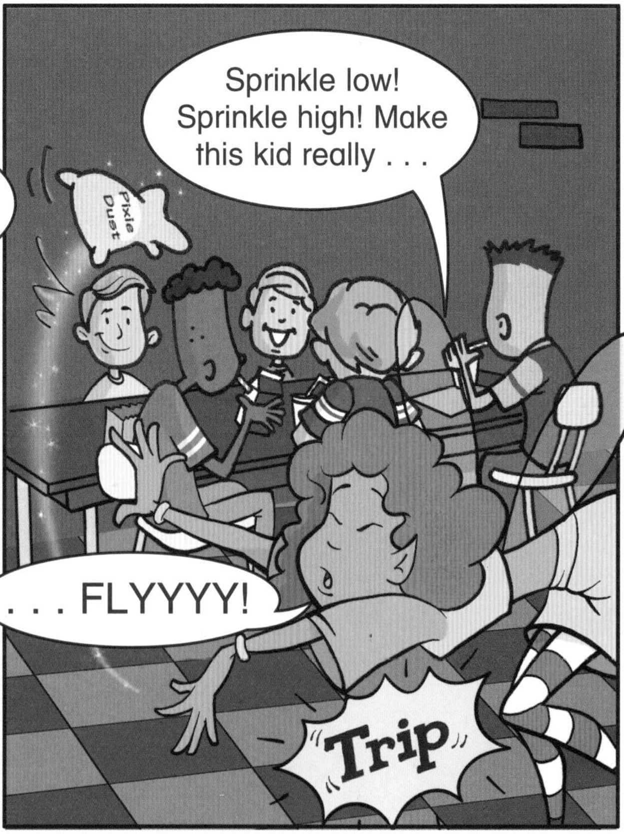
Sprinkle low! Sprinkle high! Make this kid really . . .
Pixie Dust
. . . FLYYYY!
Trip

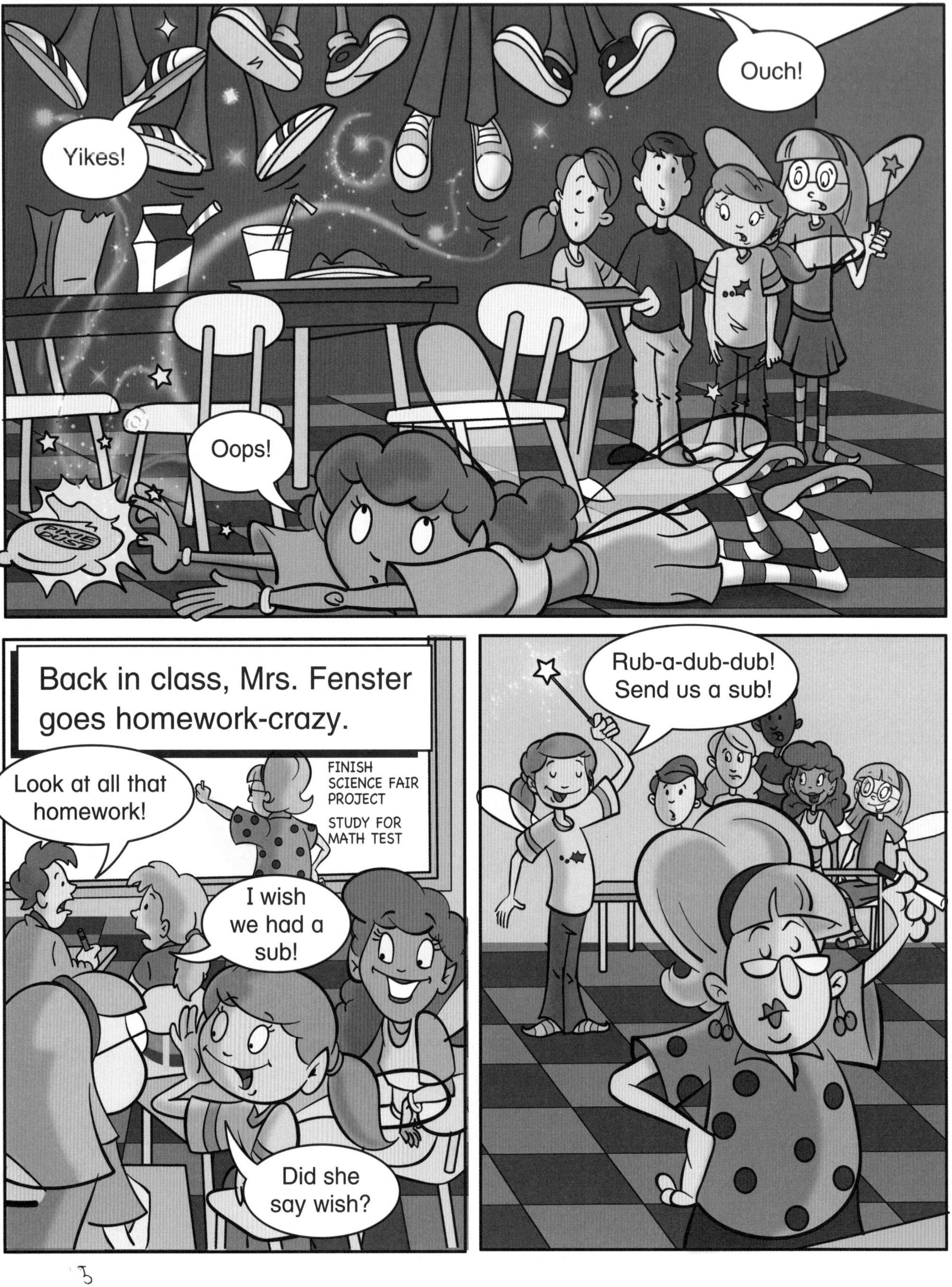

Yikes!
Ouch!
Oops!
PIXIE DUST
Back in class, Mrs. Fenster goes homework-crazy.
Look at all that homework!
FINISH SCIENCE FAIR PROJECT
STUDY FOR MATH TEST
I wish we had a sub!
Did she say wish?
Rub-a-dub-dub! Send us a sub!

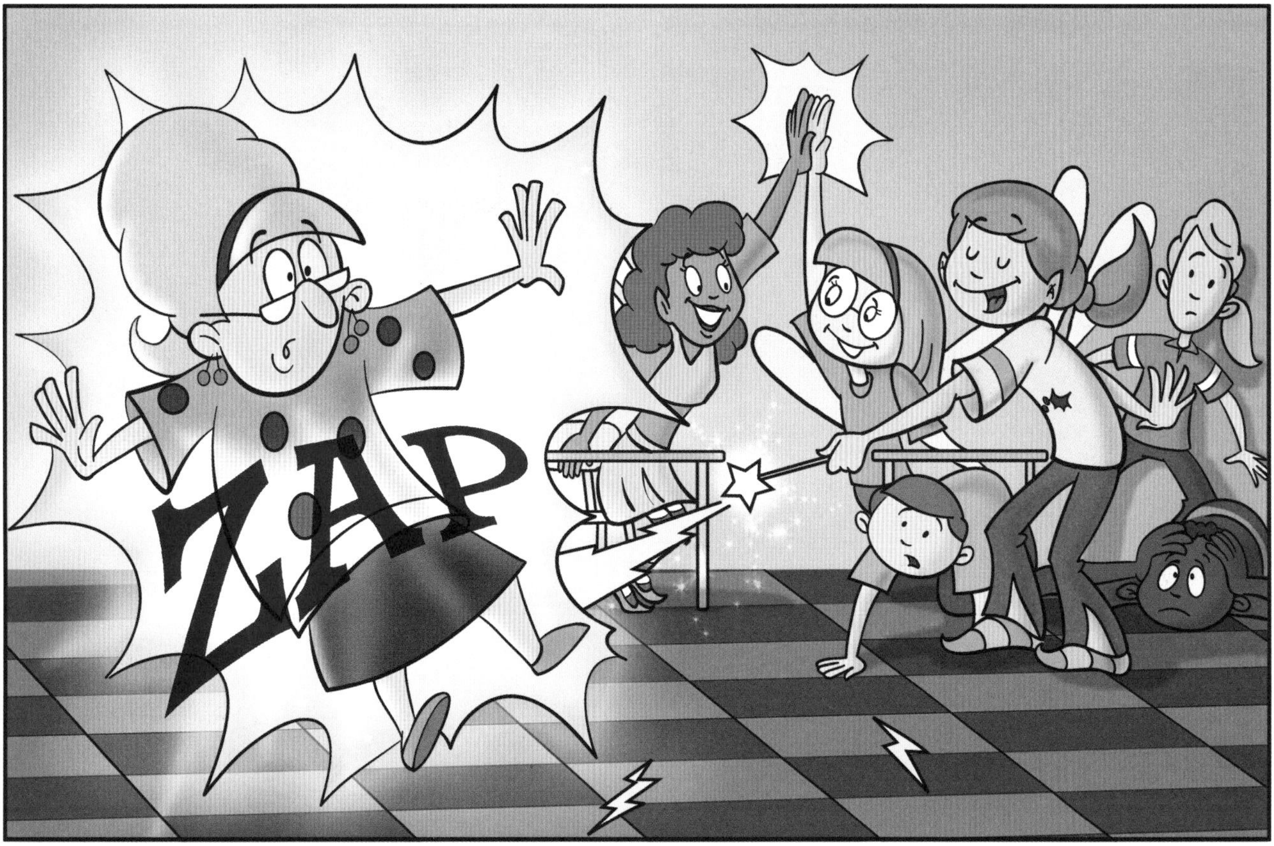
ZAP

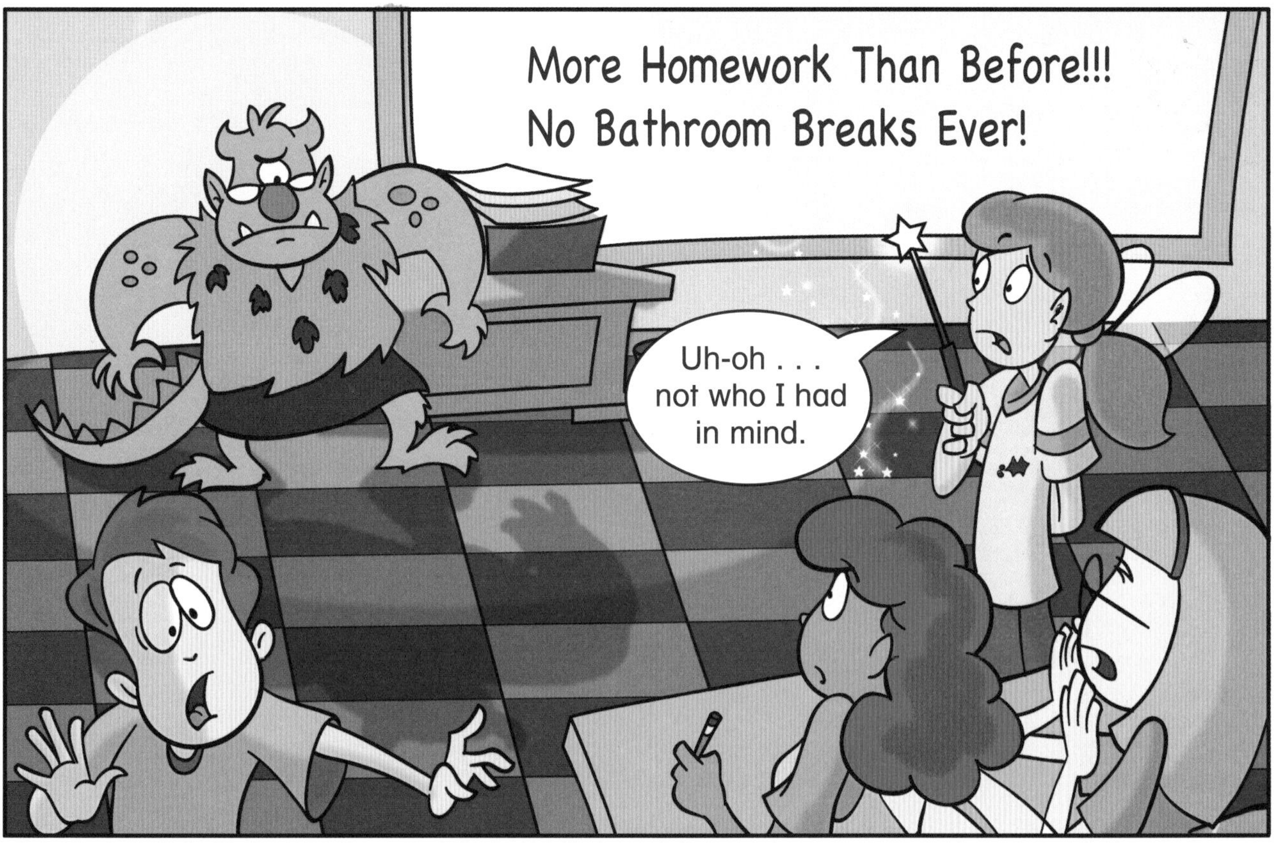
More Homework Than Before!!!
No Bathroom Breaks Ever!
Uh-oh . . . not who I had in mind.

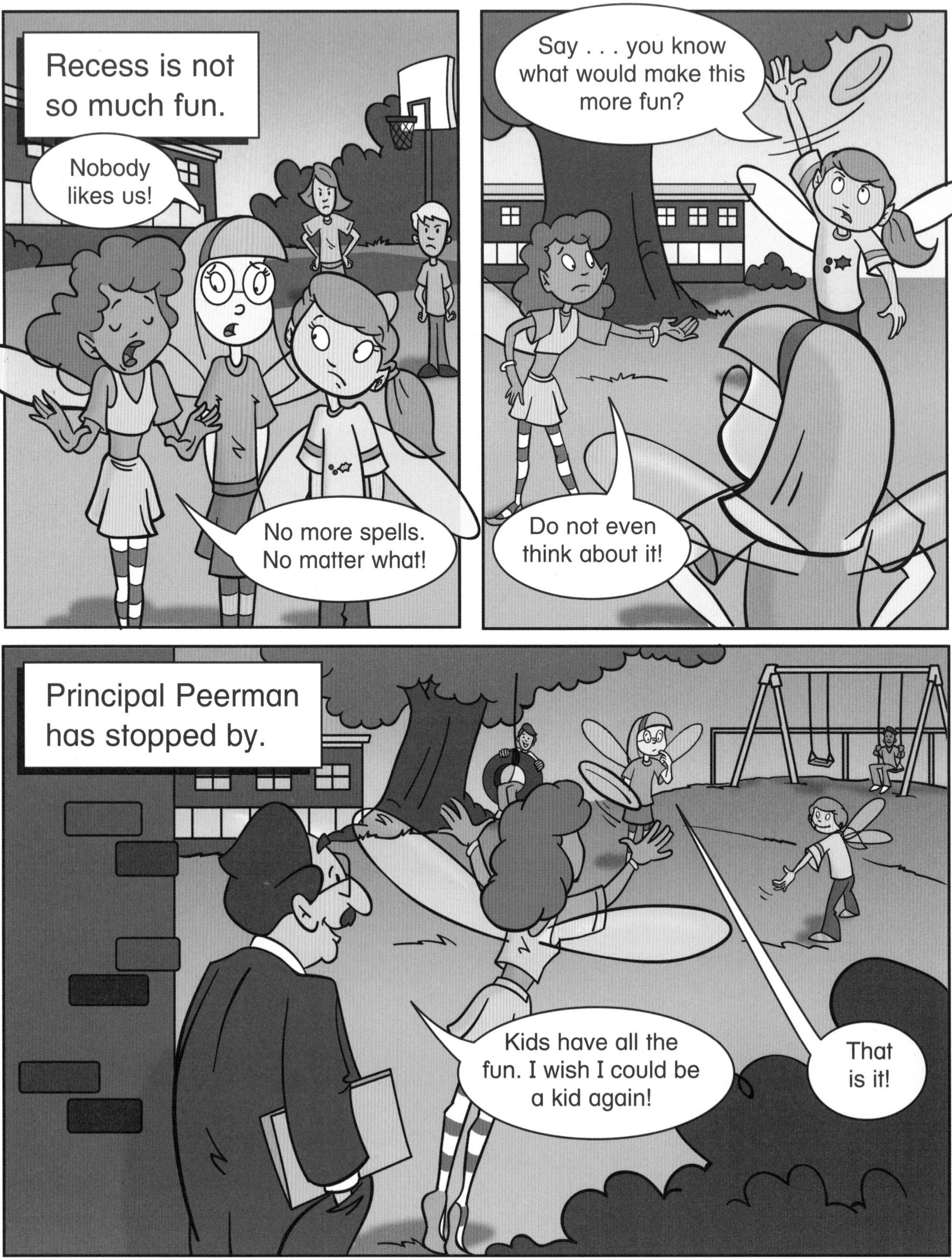
Recess is not so much fun.
Nobody likes us!
No more spells. No matter what!
Say . . . you know what would make this more fun?
Do not even think about it!
Principal Peerman has stopped by.
Kids have all the fun. I wish I could be a kid again!
That is it!

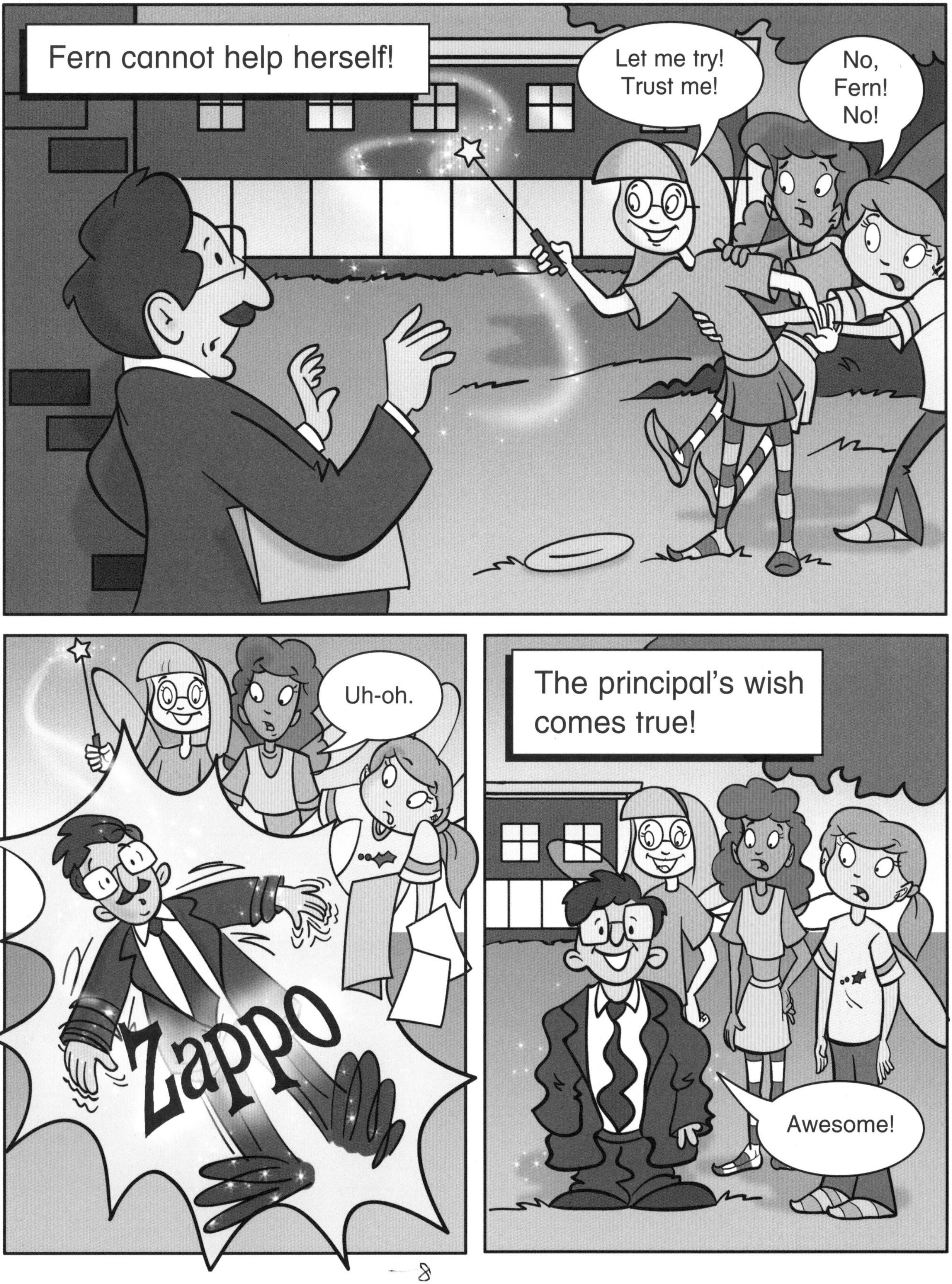
Fern cannot help herself!
Let me try! Trust me!
No, Fern! No!
Uh-oh.
Zappo
The principal's wish comes true!
Awesome!

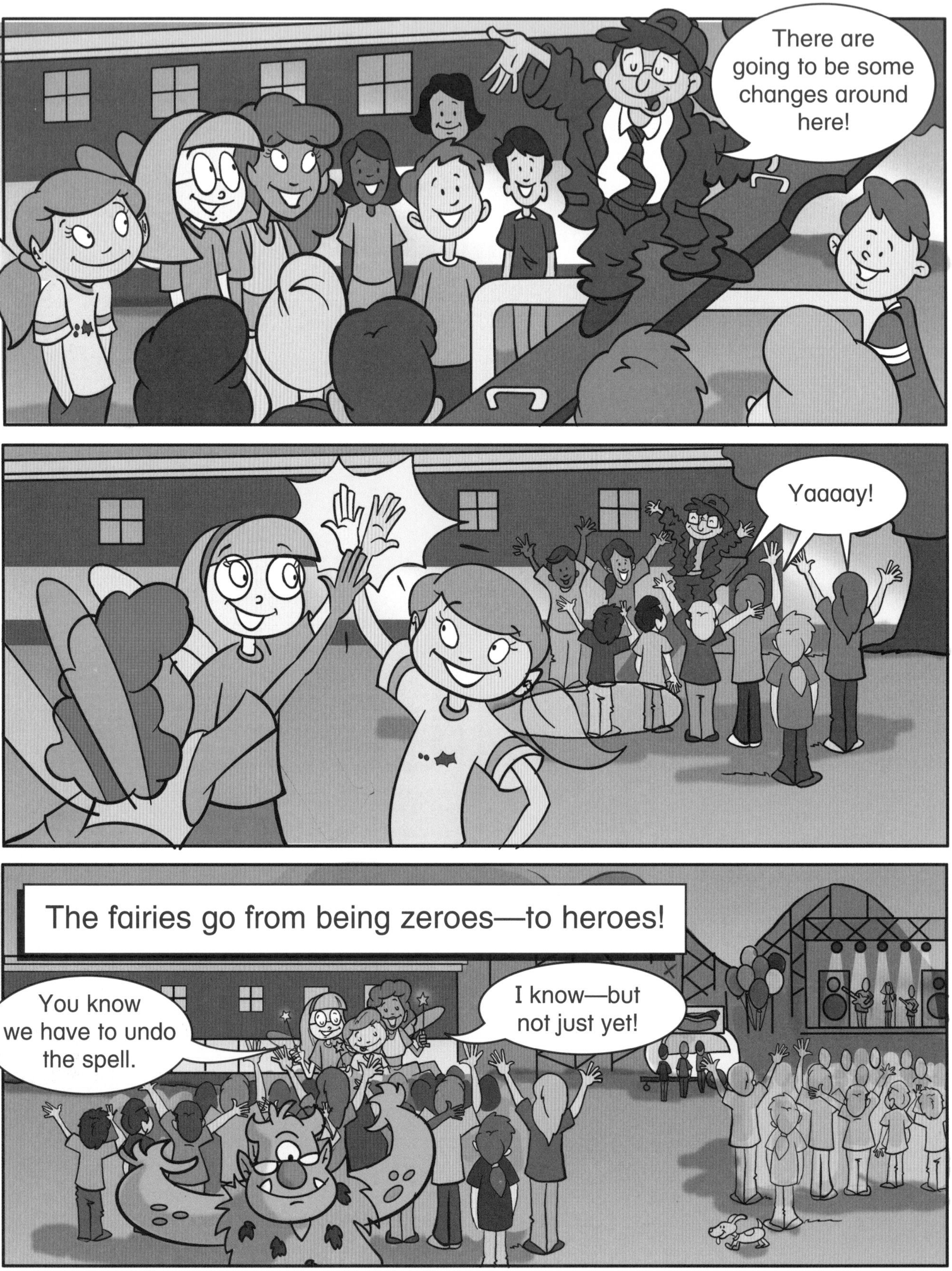
There are going to be some changes around here!
Yaaaay!
The fairies go from being zeroes—to heroes!
You know we have to undo the spell.
I know—but not just yet!

YOU WISH!

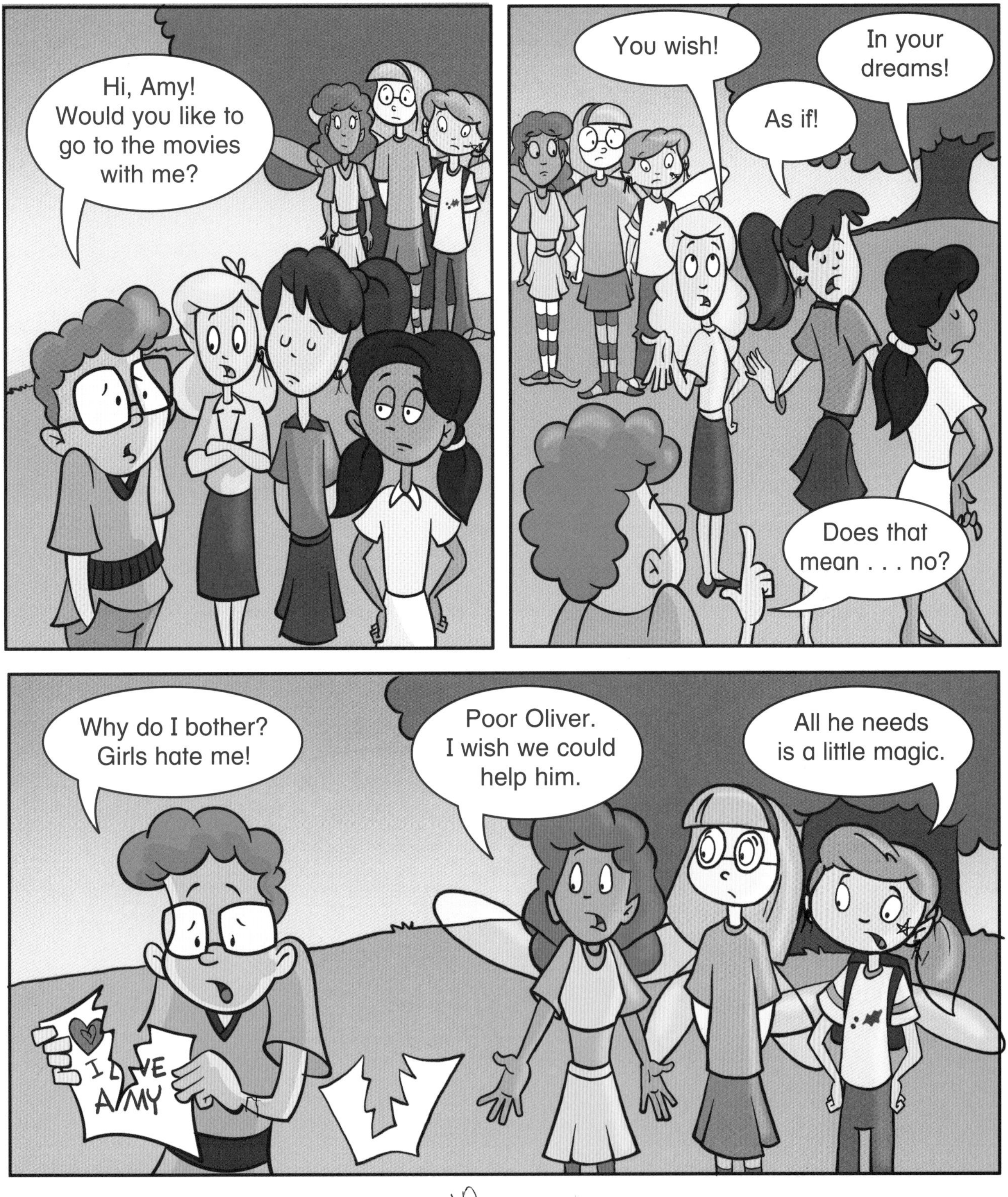
Hi, Amy! Would you like to go to the movies with me?
You wish!
As if!
In your dreams!
Does that mean . . . no?
Why do I bother? Girls hate me!
Poor Oliver. I wish we could help him.
All he needs is a little magic.
I LOVE AMY

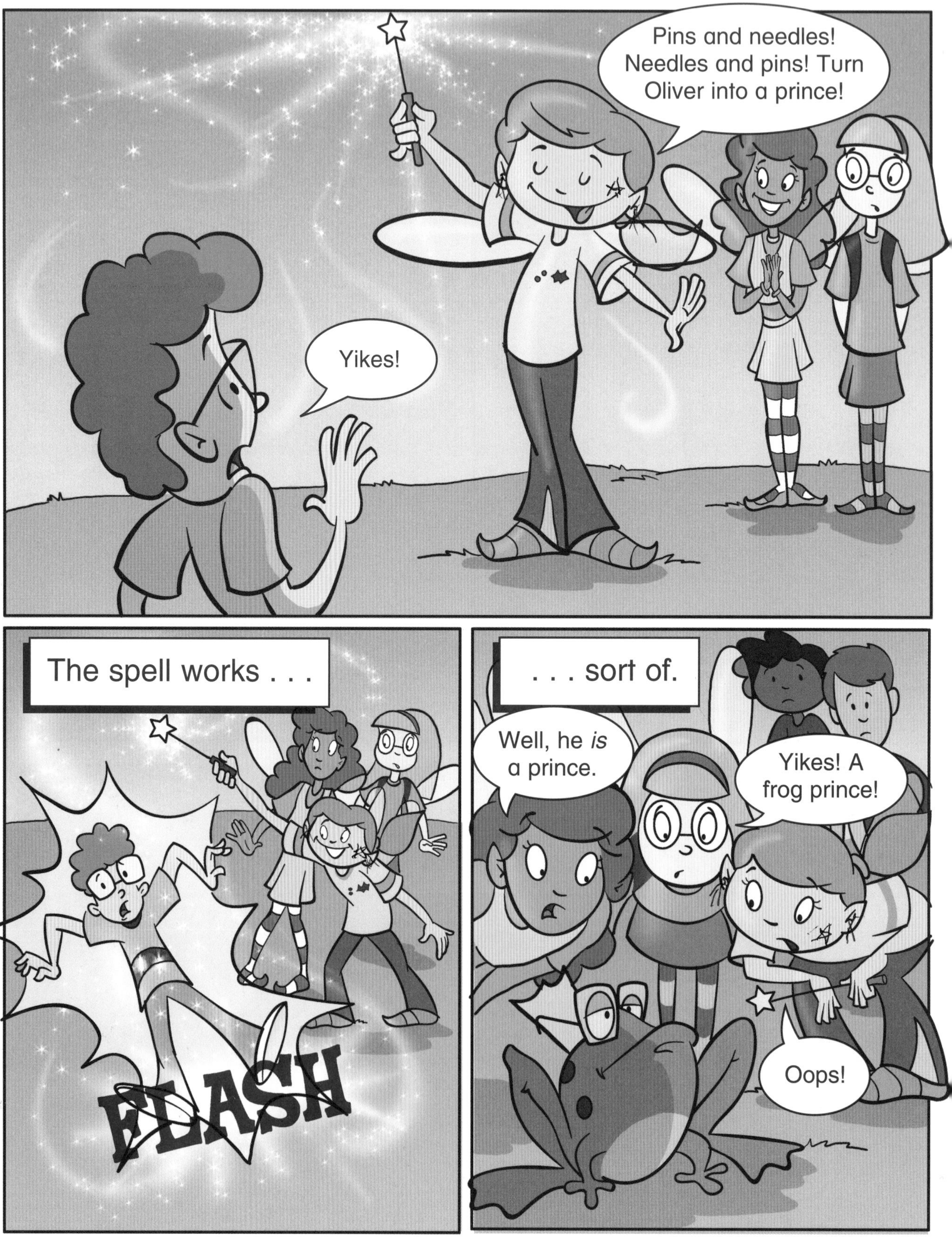
Pins and needles! Needles and pins! Turn Oliver into a prince!
Yikes!
The spell works . . .
FLASH
. . . sort of.
Well, he *is* a prince.
Yikes! A frog prince!
Oops!

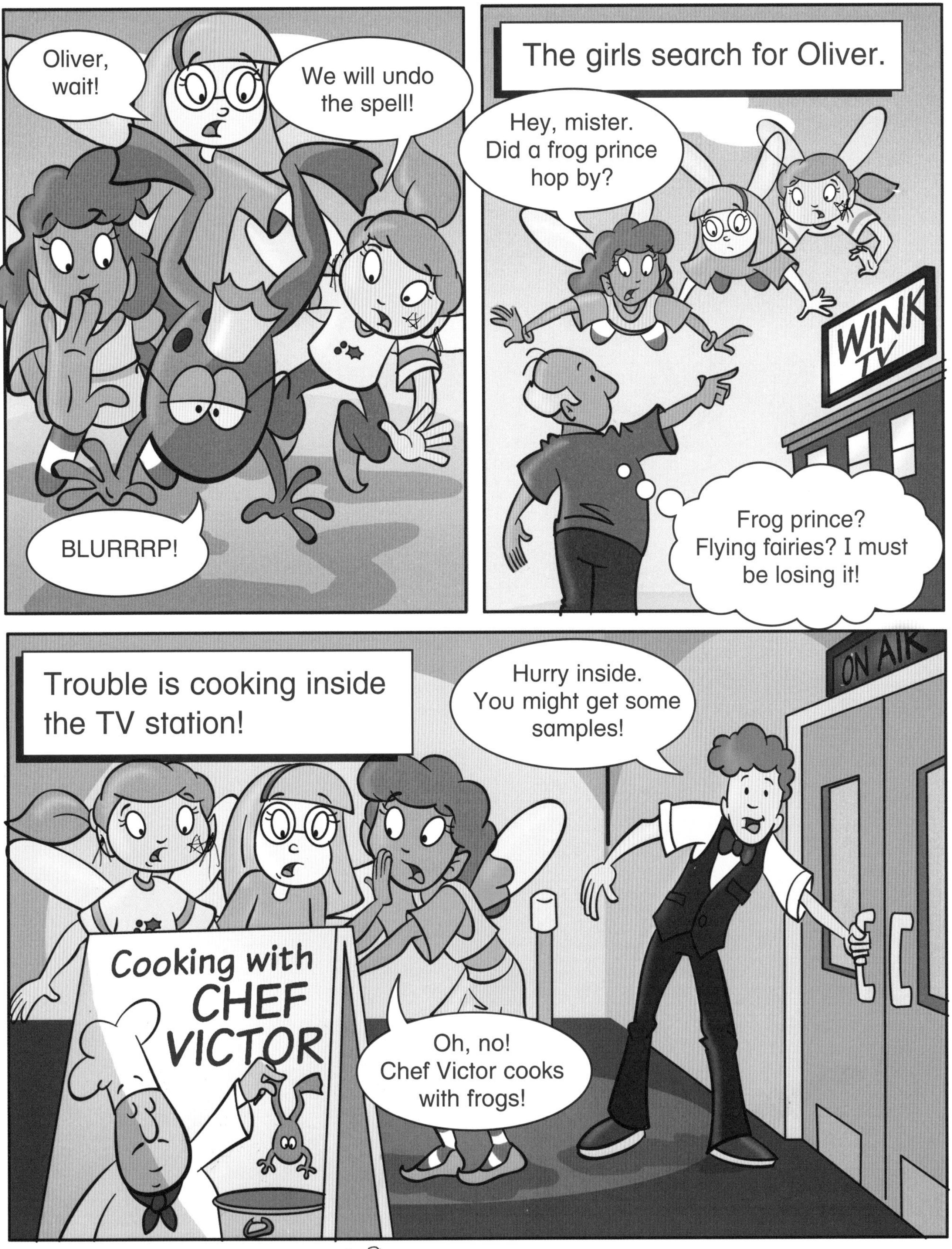
Oliver, wait!
We will undo the spell!
BLURRRP!
The girls search for Oliver.
Hey, mister. Did a frog prince hop by?
WINK TV
Frog prince? Flying fairies? I must be losing it!
Trouble is cooking inside the TV station!
Hurry inside. You might get some samples!
ON AIR
Cooking with CHEF VICTOR
Oh, no! Chef Victor cooks with frogs!

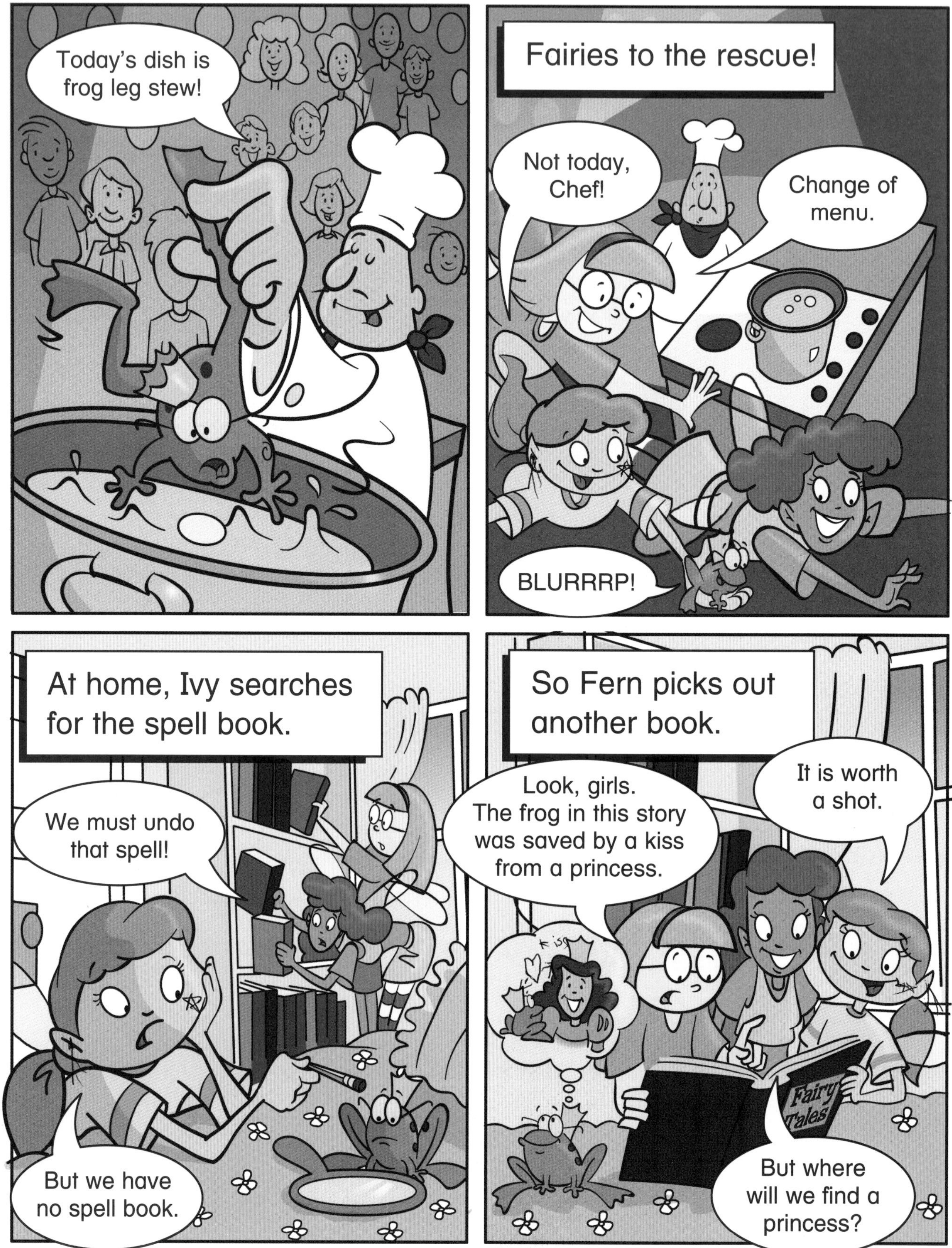
Today's dish is frog leg stew!
Fairies to the rescue!
Not today, Chef!
Change of menu.
BLURRRP!
At home, Ivy searches for the spell book.
We must undo that spell!
But we have no spell book.
So Fern picks out another book.
Look, girls. The frog in this story was saved by a kiss from a princess.
It is worth a shot.
Fairy Tales
But where will we find a princess?

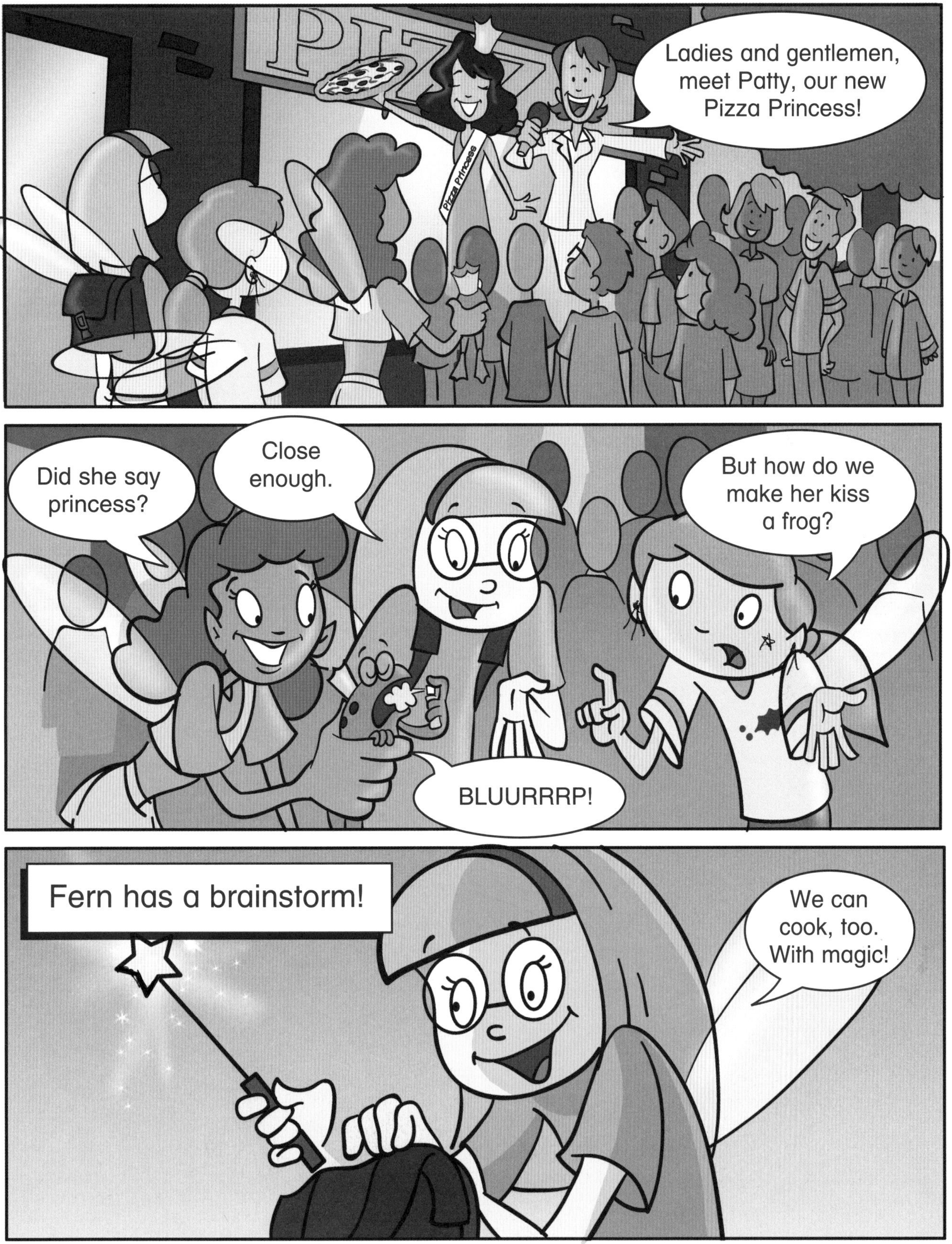
Ladies and gentlemen, meet Patty, our new Pizza Princess!
Pizza Princess
Did she say princess?
Close enough.
But how do we make her kiss a frog?
BLUURRRP!
Fern has a brainstorm!
We can cook, too. With magic!

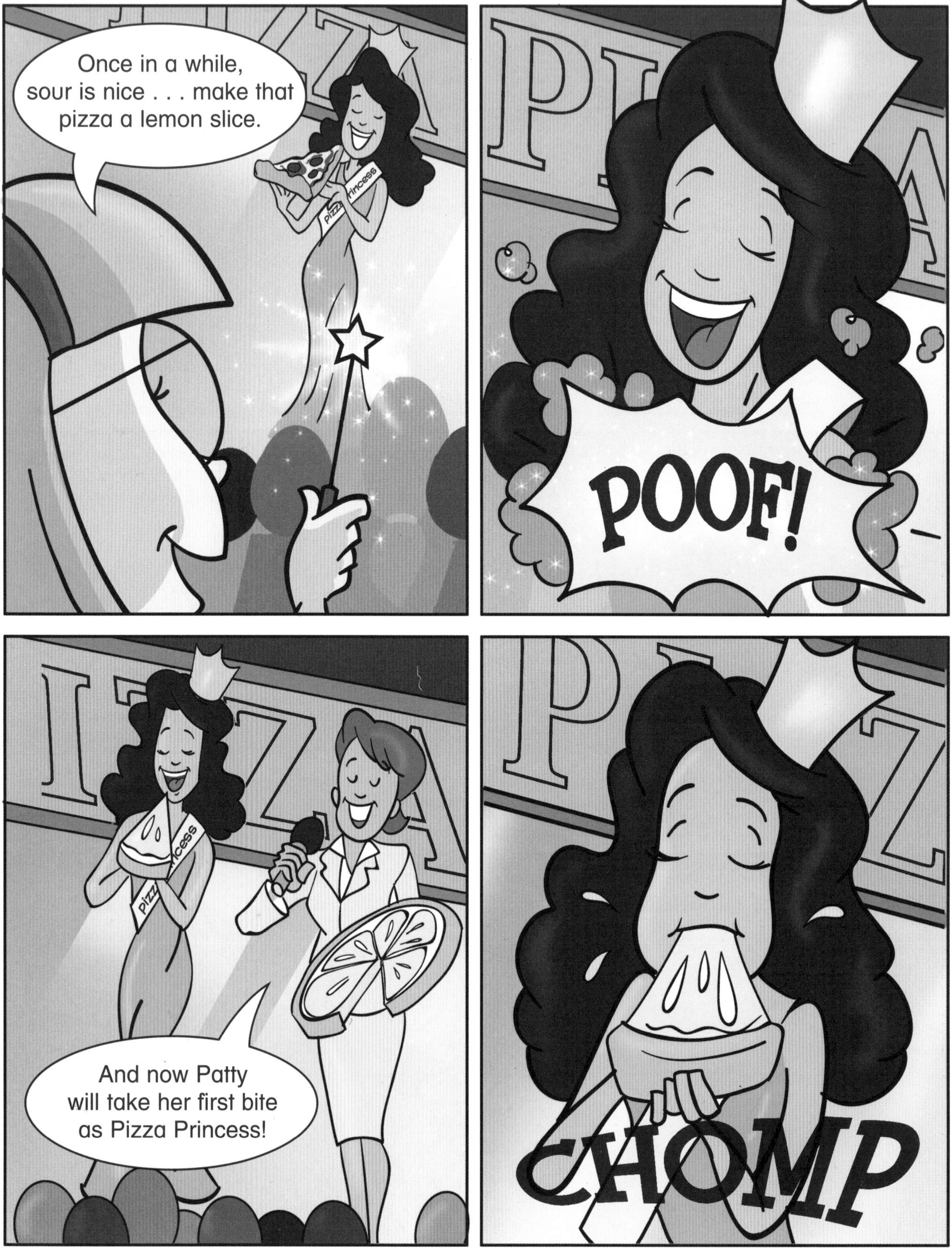
Once in a while, sour is nice . . . make that pizza a lemon slice.
POOF!
And now Patty will take her first bite as Pizza Princess!
CHOMP

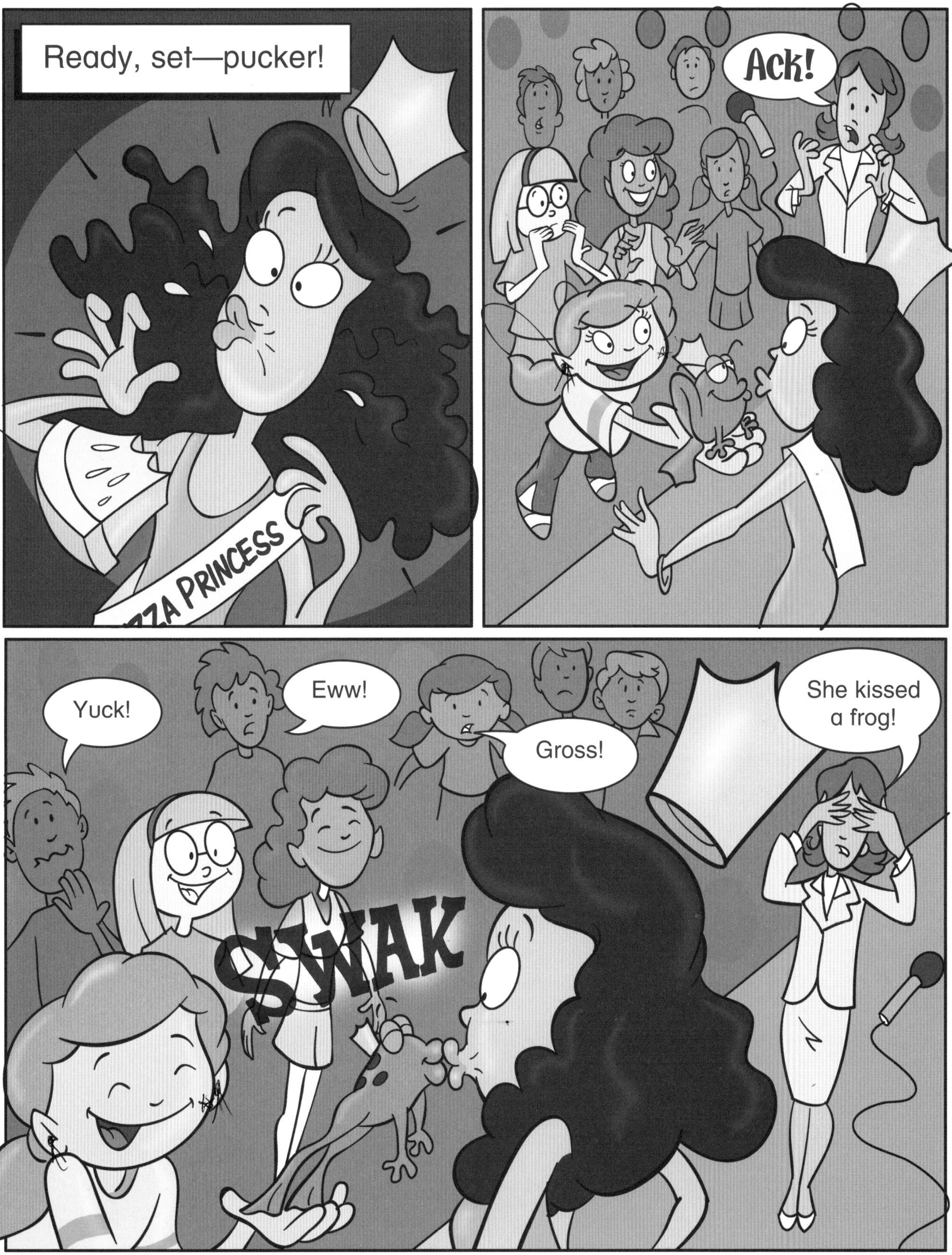
Ready, set—pucker!
PIZZA PRINCESS
Ack!
Yuck!
Eww!
Gross!
She kissed a frog!
SWAK

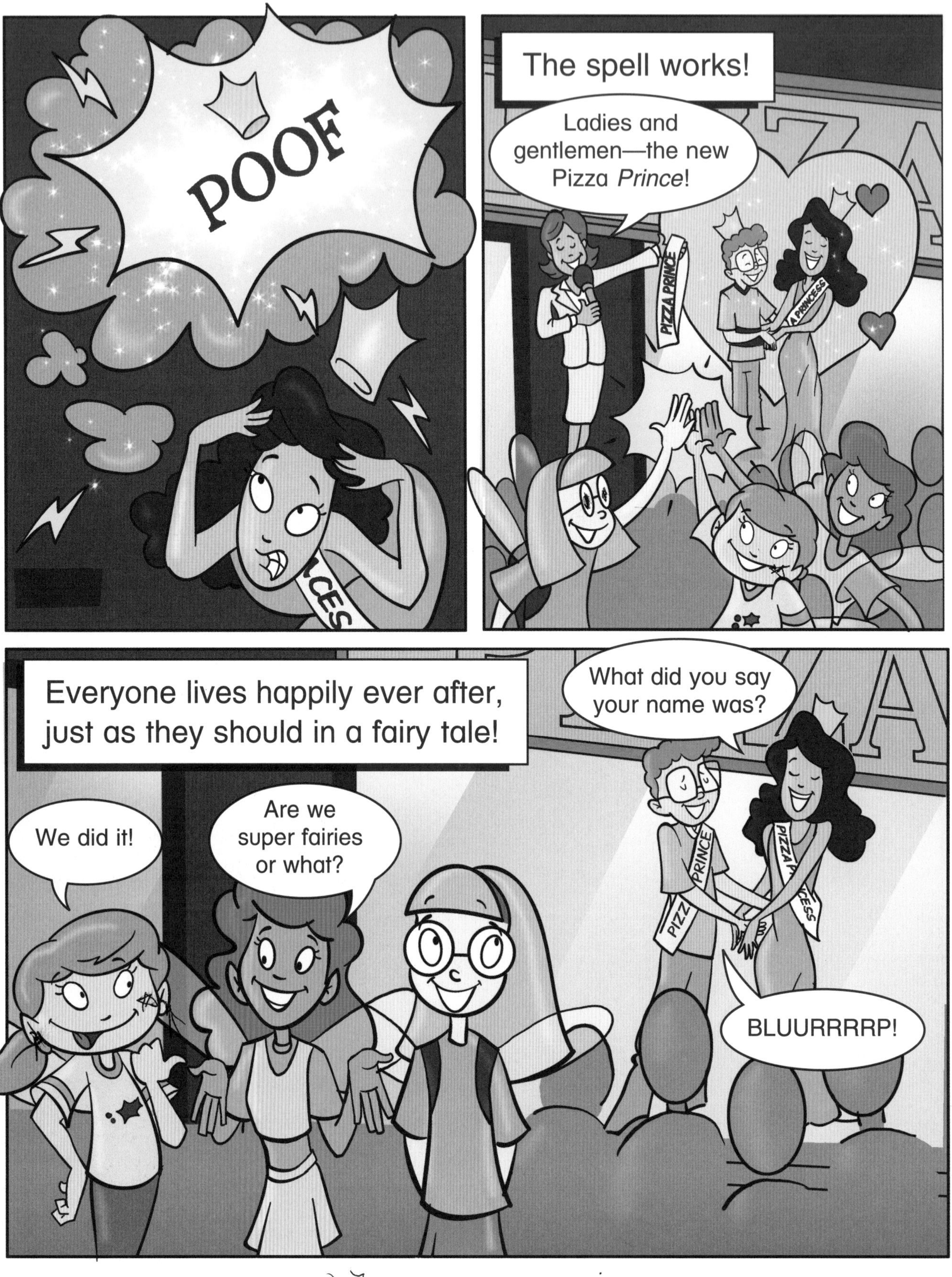
POOF
The spell works!
Ladies and gentlemen—the new Pizza *Prince*!
PIZZA PRINCE
A PRINCESS
Everyone lives happily ever after, just as they should in a fairy tale!
What did you say your name was?
We did it!
Are we super fairies or what?
BLUURRRRP!

MIND GAMES

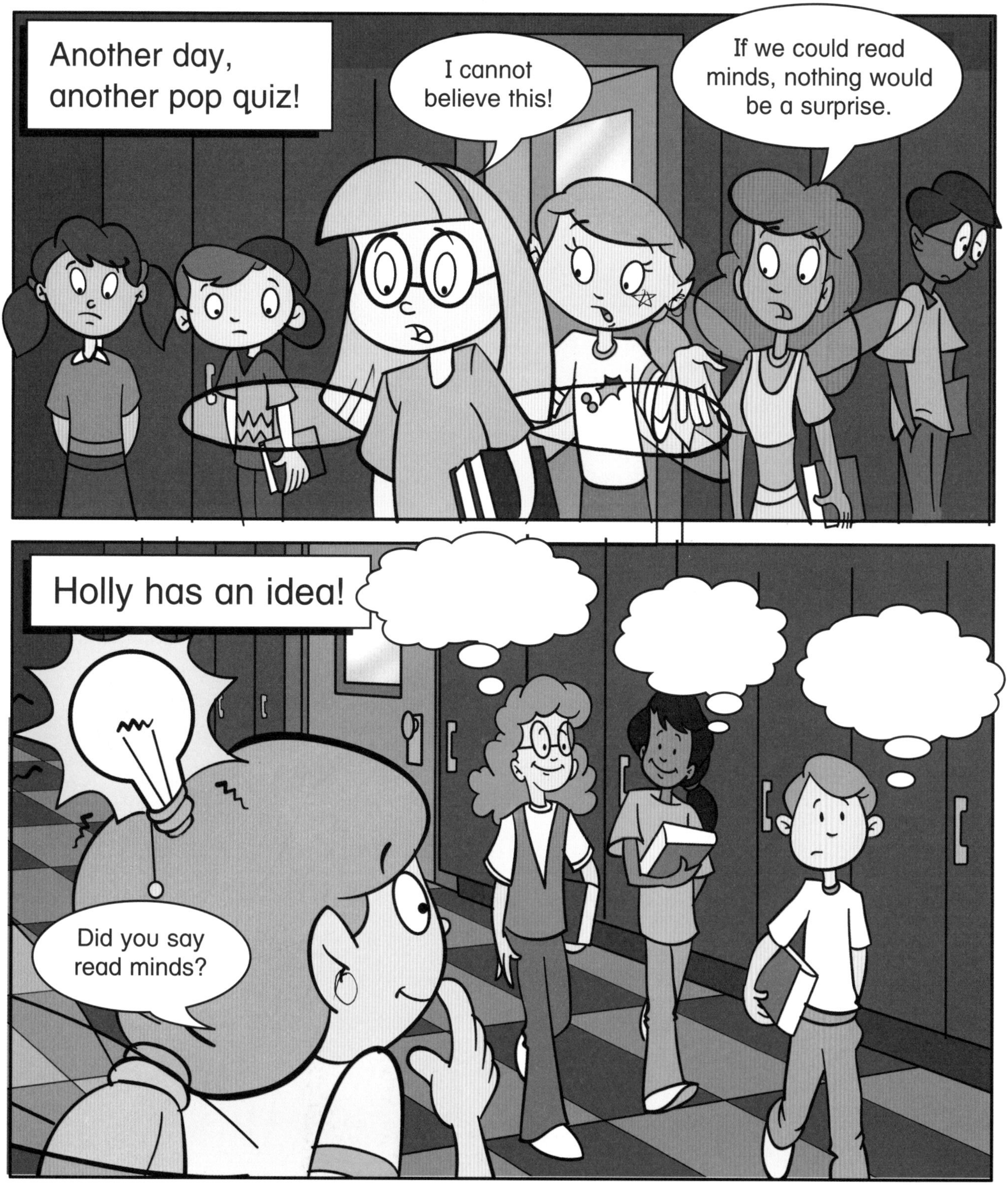
Another day, another pop quiz!
I cannot believe this!
If we could read minds, nothing would be a surprise.
Holly has an idea!
Did you say read minds?

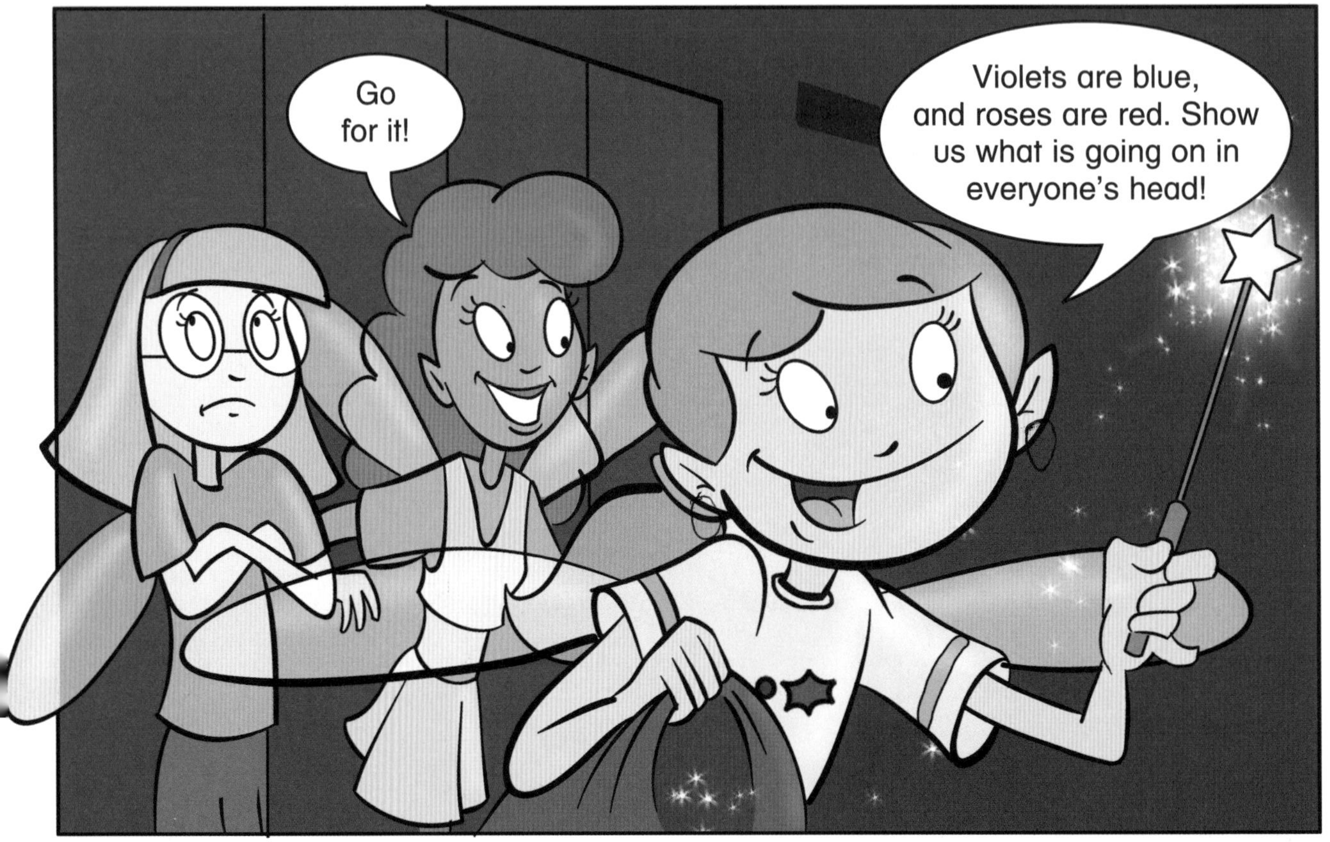
Go for it!
Violets are blue, and roses are red. Show us what is going on in everyone's head!

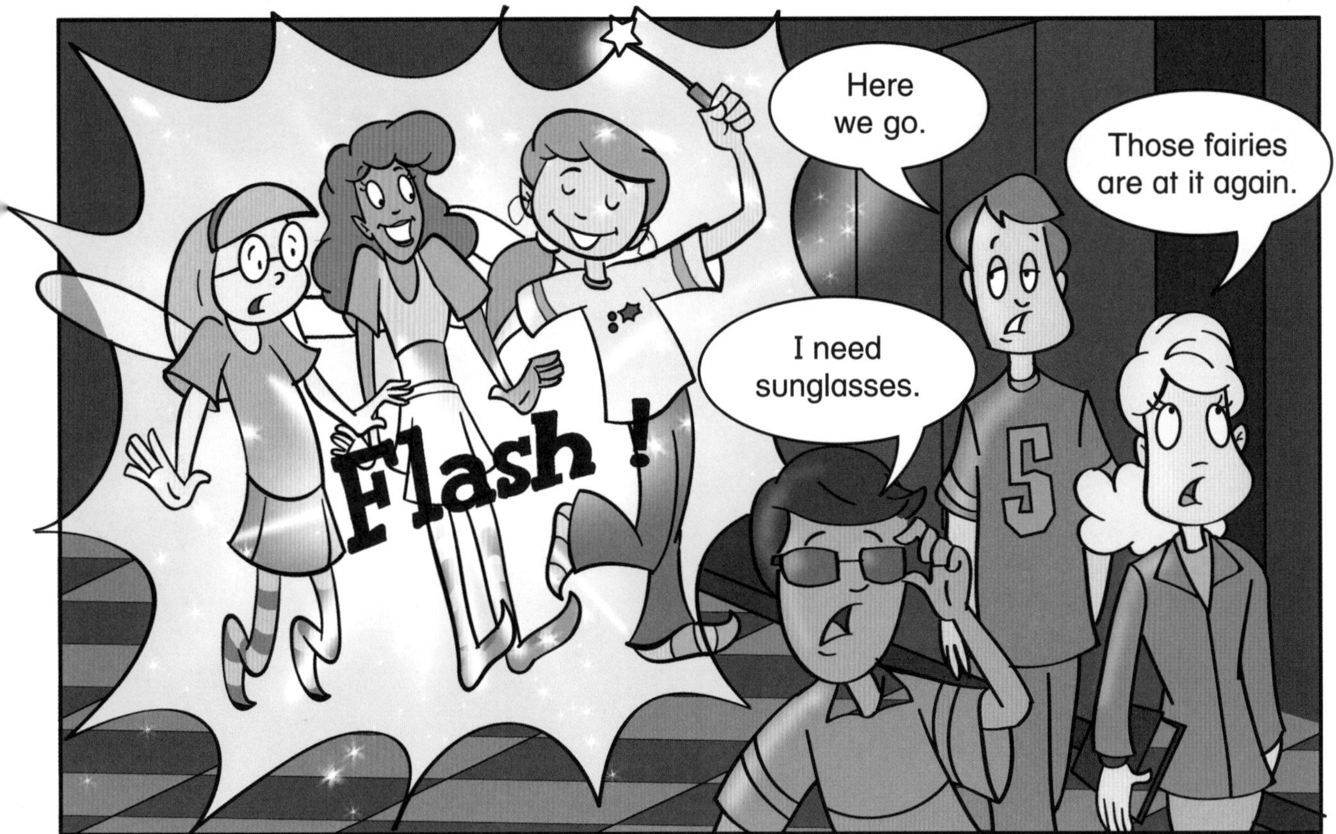
Here we go.
Those fairies are at it again.
I need sunglasses.
Flash!

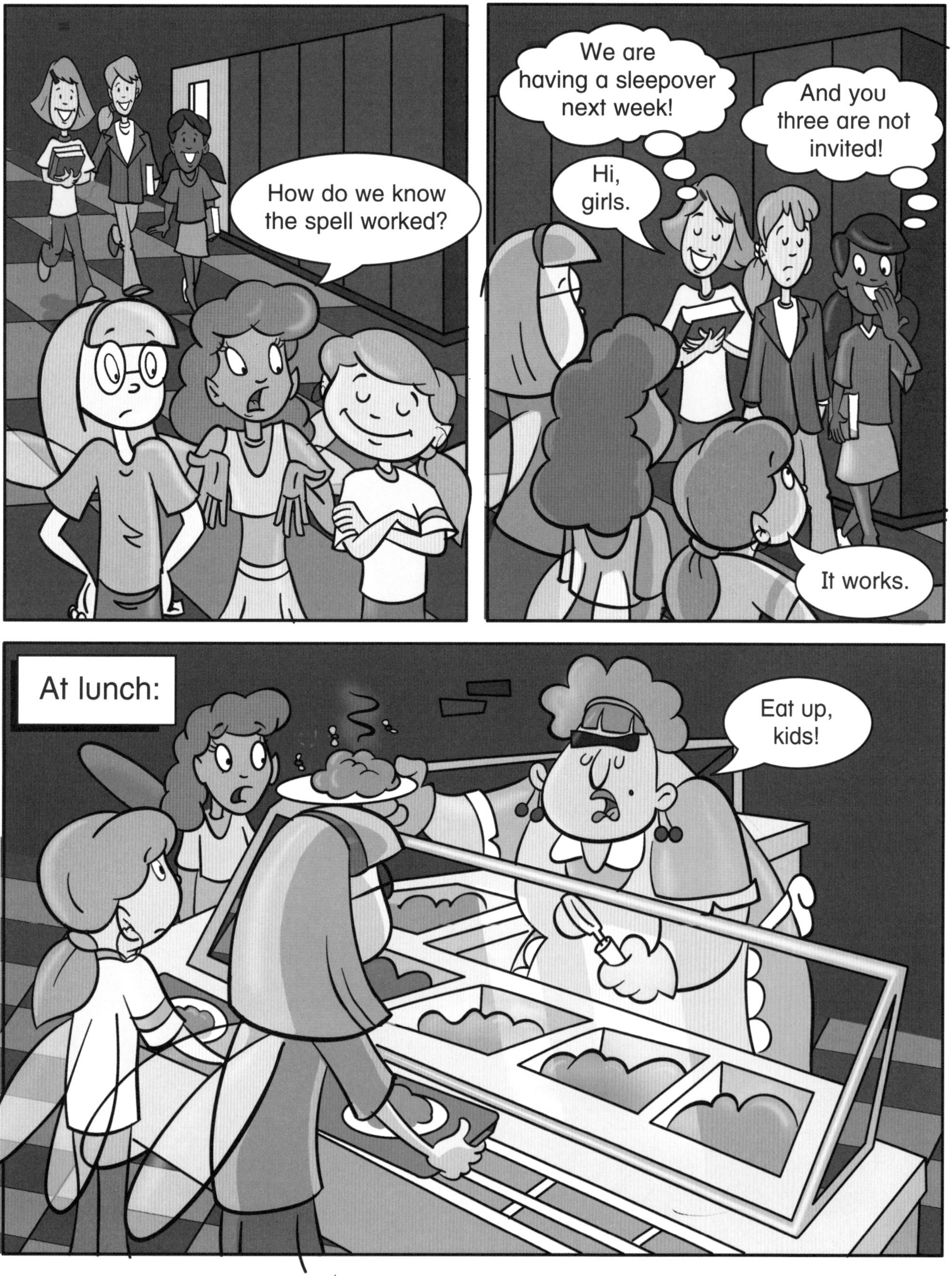
How do we know the spell worked?
Hi, girls.
We are having a sleepover next week!
And you three are not invited!
It works.
At lunch:
Eat up, kids!

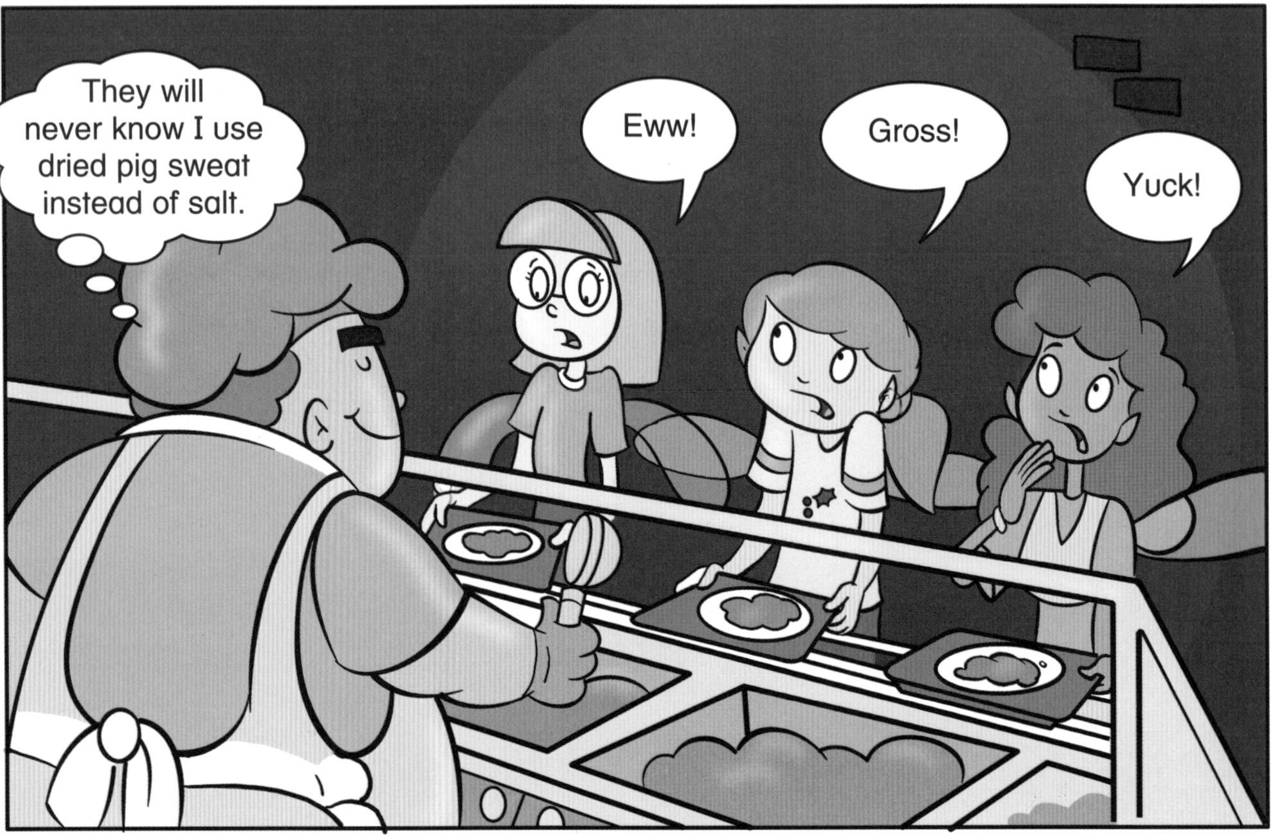
They will never know I use dried pig sweat instead of salt.
Eww!
Gross!
Yuck!

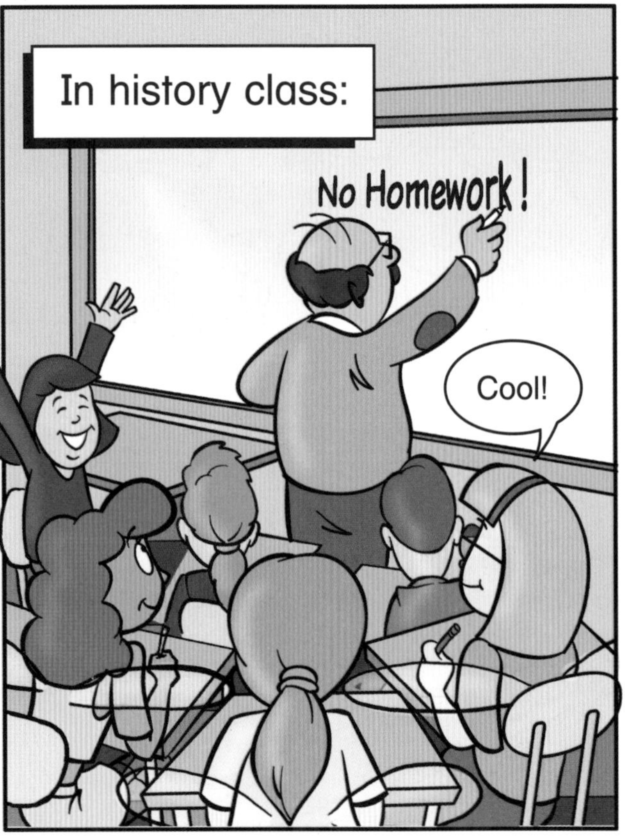
In history class:
No Homework!
Cool!

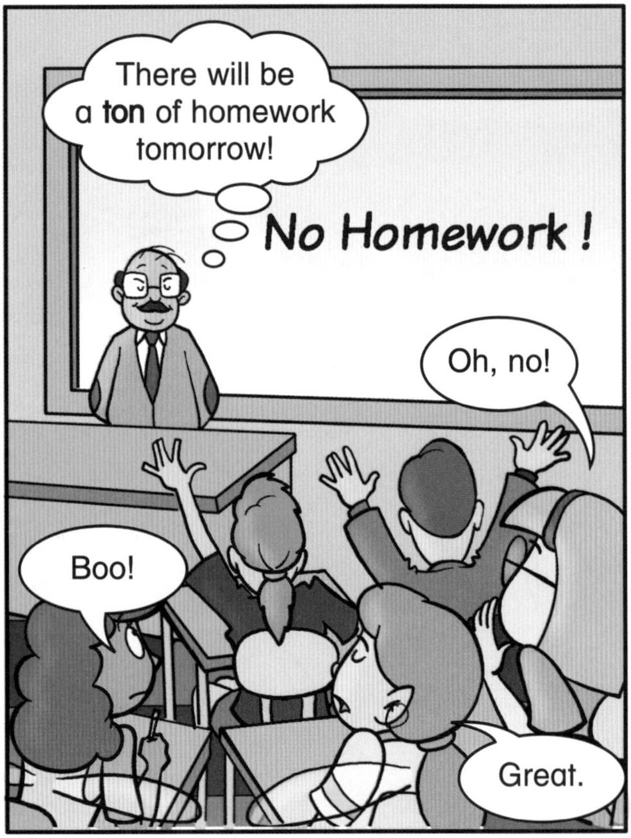
There will be a **ton** of homework tomorrow!
No Homework!
Oh, no!
Boo!
Great.

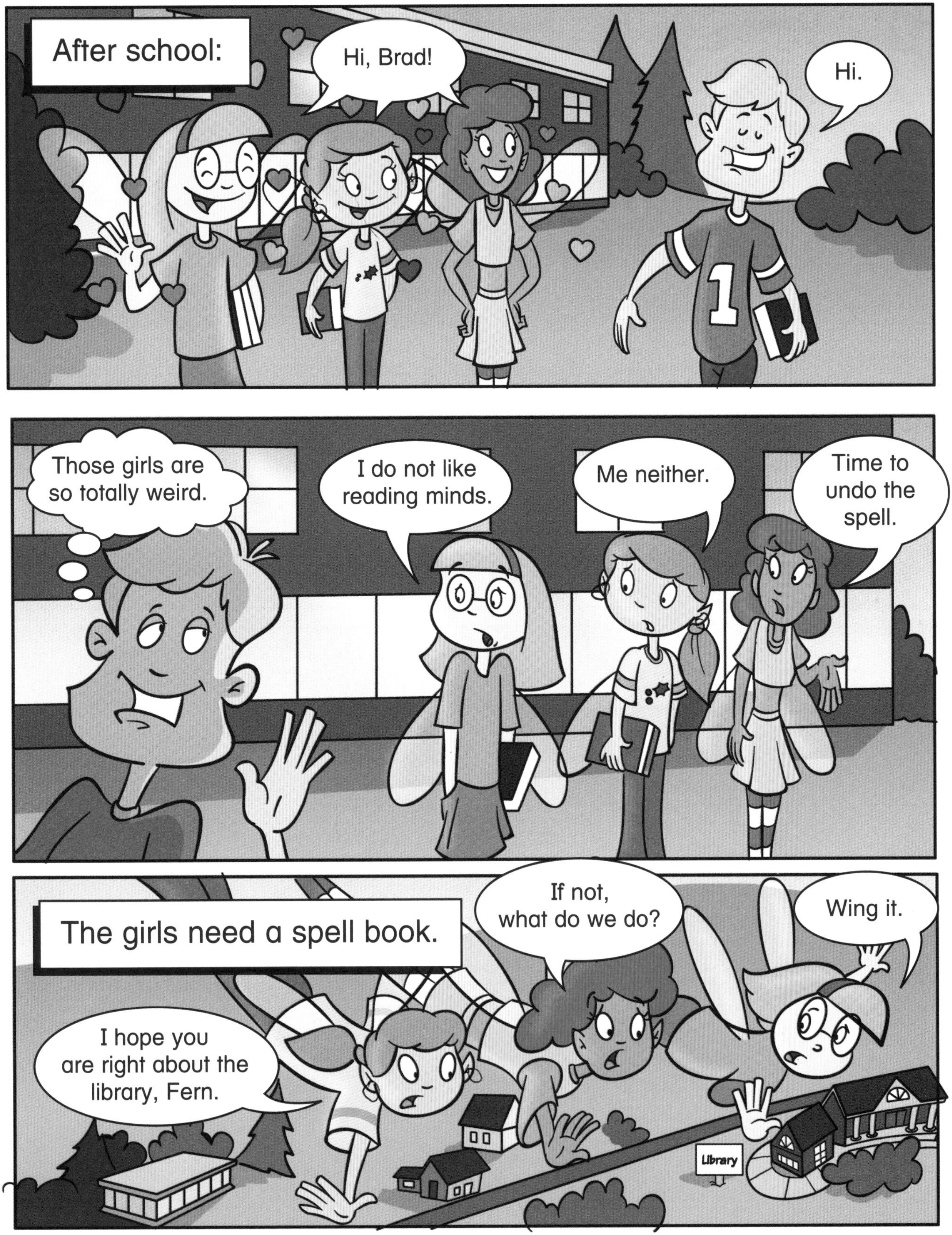
After school:
Hi, Brad!
Hi.
Those girls are so totally weird.
I do not like reading minds.
Me neither.
Time to undo the spell.
The girls need a spell book.
If not, what do we do?
Wing it.
I hope you are right about the library, Fern.
Library

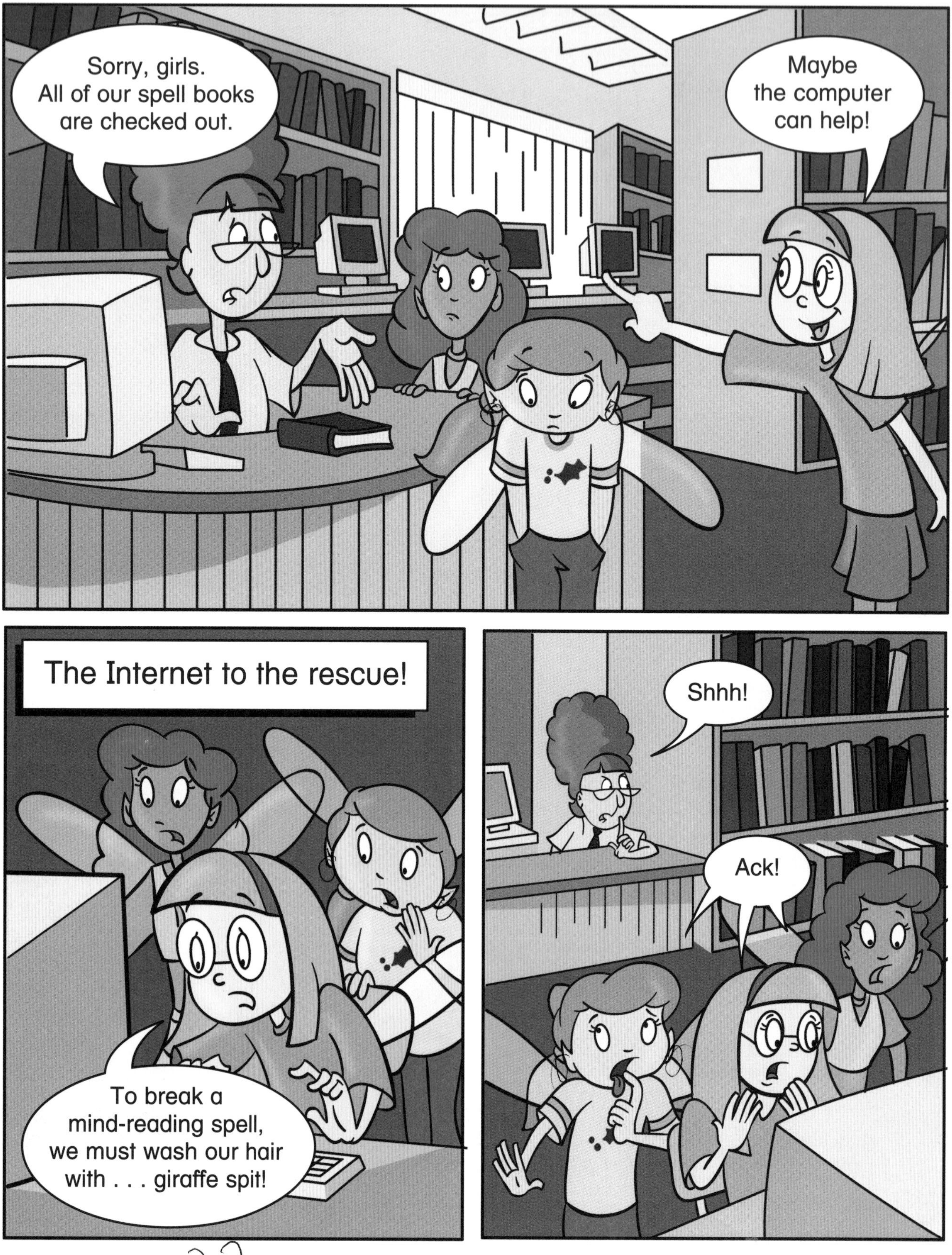
Sorry, girls. All of our spell books are checked out.
Maybe the computer can help!
The Internet to the rescue!
To break a mind-reading spell, we must wash our hair with . . . giraffe spit!
Shhh!
Ack!

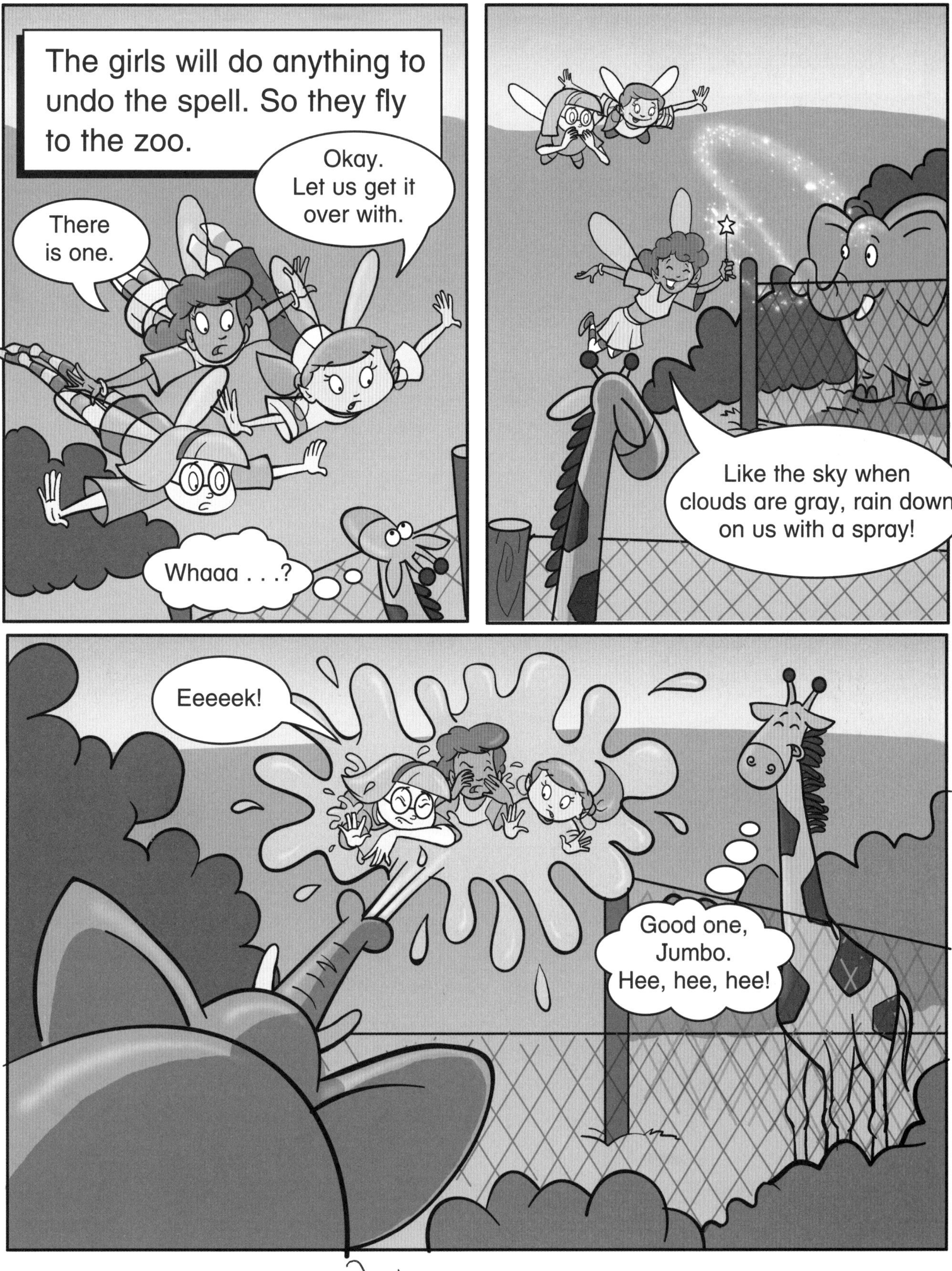
The girls will do anything to undo the spell. So they fly to the zoo.
There is one.
Okay. Let us get it over with.
Whaaa . . .?
Like the sky when clouds are gray, rain down on us with a spray!
Eeeeek!
Good one, Jumbo. Hee, hee, hee!

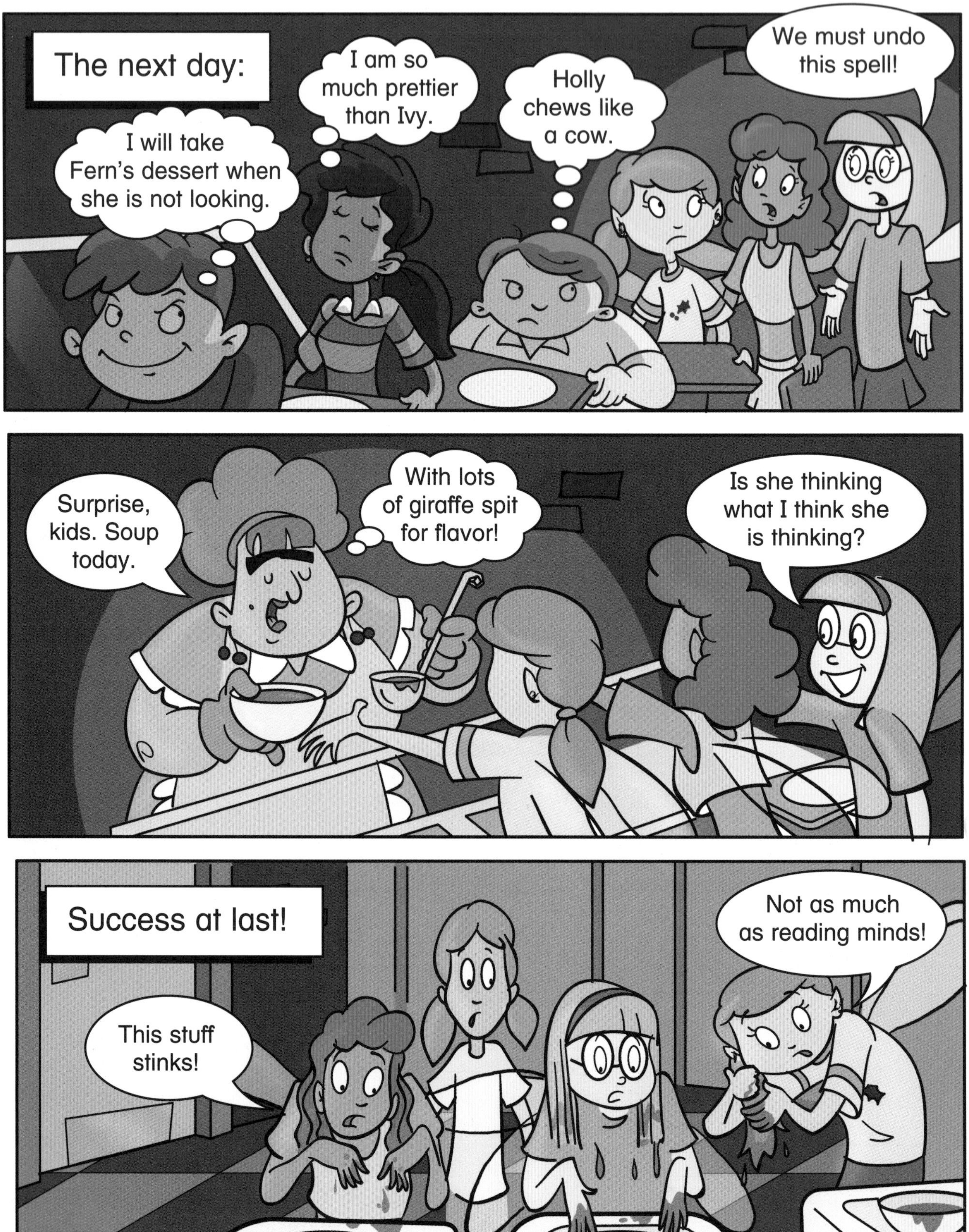

The next day:
I will take Fern's dessert when she is not looking.
I am so much prettier than Ivy.
Holly chews like a cow.
We must undo this spell!
Surprise, kids. Soup today.
With lots of giraffe spit for flavor!
Is she thinking what I think she is thinking?
Success at last!
This stuff stinks!
Not as much as reading minds!